Praise for *Roy of the Rovers*

"It has **everything that a football fan needs...** match day action, local club rivalry, modern football politics, trials, crunching tackles, tricks, misses and goals. It also has everything that today's children need as they grow up. It is jam-packed with positive role models, girls' involvement in Women's Football, respect, mental well-being, good work ethic, education and aspiration." – *Books for Topics*

"Packs a lot of punch in its short and simple to read pages... **It captures the feel of playing and having a passion for football** at an early age very well. More than that it sets out the stall of the new Roy Race, his family background, his friends and enemies, where he lives and his work ethic." – *Comic Scene Magazine*

"**I give it 5,000,000 stars**! I recommend it to 9+ football fans but also non-football fans. I'm not a football fan but I still really enjoyed reading this book. Look out for the graphic novels and the rest of the series. Amazing!" – *The Book Brothers*

"**Football-lovers will love the description of on-pitch action** which is pacy yet satisfyingly detailed. This is a book that I am looking forward to putting on the shelves at school – I know already that it will be a popular title amongst our football-loving children

First published 2019 by Rebellion Publishing Ltd,
Riverside House, Osney Mead, Oxford, OX2 0ES, UK

ISBN: 978 1 78108 685 8

10 9 8 7 6 5 4 3 2 1

A CIP catalogue record for this book is available
from the British Library.

Printed in Denmark

Creative Director and CEO: Jason Kingsley
Chief Technical Officer: Chris Kinglsey
Head of Publishing: Ben Smith
Editor: Rob Power   Design: Sam Gretton   Cover image: Lisa Henke

Follow us:

royoftheroversofficial   royoftheroversofficial   royoftherovers

www.royoftherovers.com   info@royoftherovers.com

To Rob Power, my first Roy editor

The story so far...

ROY RACE IS a totally normal sixteen-year-old; he studies at college, fights with his little sister – and plays centre forward for Melchester Rovers.

Ok, so he's not *that* normal.

And while it might sound like Roy's got the perfect life, he's got a lot on his plate.

He's had to overcome injuries, social media scandals, the perils of fame and the pressure of performing as one of the best young footballers in the country.

Plus, things aren't exactly easy at home. Roy cares for his disabled father, helps his over-worked mother out as much as he can, *and* coaches his little sister Rocky as she attempts to start a football career of her own.

Of course, all of this would be a lot easier if Melchester Rovers were the biggest club in the country.

But they're not.

Although they scraped promotion to League One last season, Melchester Rovers are still owned by money-grabbing businessman Barry Cleaver, who refuses to invest in the club. Now that Rovers are on the up, Cleaver is looking for opportunities to make money quickly, and his squad full of talented young players – including Roy – could be just the ticket.

For now, all Roy has to do is train hard in pre-season, and focus on his quest to return Melchester Rovers to footballing glory. Sounds easy, right?

ROY RACE RAN steadily, picking his way down the hill from his house to warm up his muscles.

When he was on the canal path at the bottom of the hill, he went for it: half a mile of flat track to stretch out his legs before he reached Mel Park, dodging overgrown summer bushes as he sprinted. He enjoyed the rush of air past his ears as he ran hard. His legs felt good. His body felt good. He'd kept himself fit during the close season.

He was excited, too. Today the team would find out where they'd be going on the Rovers' pre-season tour.

Roy finished with a quick sprint across the car park at the front of Mel Park, the Melchester Rovers stadium. That box of yellow and red corrugated iron with a floodlight sprouting in each corner. And, there, he saw a queue of people at the ticket office.

A queue, because today was a big day. Every other year of his life he'd been in that queue, breathless with anticipation as he waited to collect his season ticket to watch his heroes, the Melchester Rovers players.

Now Roy *was* one of those players. And he still couldn't believe it. Every day he woke up unable to accept it was really happening to him.

Slowing to a jog, making sure he didn't trip on any of the tufts of grass or crumbling tarmac in the car park, Roy remembered a conversation he'd had with his teammate, Paco Diaz, when they'd achieved promotion from League Two just eight weeks ago: their hope that Paco would be allowed to wear the eleven shirt and Roy the number nine.

Roy smiled as he approached the players' entrance. It still looked shabby, still needed a new coat of paint. He wondered why the door – like the car park – had not been tidied up during the summer.

He had a good idea why. The Melchester Rovers owner and chairman – Barry Cleaver – was the reason. He was tight-fisted, and would rather the players walked in through a shabby door then spend a few quid on a pot of paint.

Near the players' entrance there was a man with a small girl waiting in the shadow of the main stand, staring hard at Roy. Roy expected to be asked for an autograph.

That was what sometimes happened now. And he was all set to be friendly and smiley, especially towards the child.

But the man did not want an autograph.

'Come to clear out your locker?' he said, scowling at Roy.

'Eh?' Roy asked.

'I said,' the man growled, his voice rising even more, 'have you just come by to collect your things?'

Roy sighed. This again. How many times did he have to tell people?

Throughout the summer break – after Melchester Rovers' playoff promotion from League Two – there had been rumours about Roy and Paco Diaz leaving Rovers.

Roy had even been introduced to the Tynecaster owner, Julio Garcia, and told him straight. No way he was leaving Mel Park. Not ever.

So why were people still asking him?

Roy took a moment to remember what his coach – Johnny Dexter – had said to him about the club's supporters: *Whatever they say to you, be polite and respectful. One day they'll love you, the next they'll hate you, but every day they pay your wages. They are the soul of the club.*

But still, Roy reflected. Shouting something like that? In front of a child?

He chose his words carefully, expressing them calmly. 'I'm one hundred per cent Melchester Rovers,' Roy said. 'I love this club. I've been coming as a fan all my life. I'm not leaving. We've just been promoted to League One. Why would I leave?'

'Not what it says on here,' the man said, stepping backwards, holding his phone up.

Roy shrugged and gazed across the car park in despair. He hated this so much: that anyone could question his love for Melchester Rovers.

Roy turned to go. He would try not to let the man and what he said worry him. As he pushed on the players' entrance door, he noticed a shiny red Aston Martin in the reserved parking bays. It was a car he'd seen before.

It belonged to football agent Alan Talbot.

The sight of that car *did* worry him. Alan Talbot was a man Roy did not trust. And he always seemed to be around just before trouble arrived.

2

A SMALL GROUP of young men, none of them over the age of twenty, met in the shadow of the main stand. All around were thousands of empty seats, upturned, just as they'd been left when Rovers had played their last game at Mel Park in May.

The Melchester Rovers squad.

In front of them the pitch looked a little dry in places. It had been a hot summer, but Roy was again surprised nothing had been done to improve the football ground since promotion. He'd assumed there would be repairs. Like outside, there had been nothing done. Mel Park looked a little… shabby.

Roy counted sixteen players, including himself. There was a sleepiness about them all. Three or four of them were clearly a little out of condition. This was Roy's first start of a season as a professional footballer. Maybe, he thought, this is normal. Maybe players let themselves go in the summer, to relax. It was

not how Roy had done it, but each to his own.

Up front – standing on track that surrounded the pitch – were two figures.

Johnny Dexter: the Melchester Rovers coach.

Frankie Pepper: the physio and conditioning coach.

There was no sign of Hot-Shot Hamish, the club's interim manager from the very end of last season. Or Mouse, the man he had replaced.

The promotion at the end of last season had been glorious, but hard too. The team manager – Kevin 'Mighty' Mouse – had been taken ill and replaced by Hot-Shot Hamish. It all came back to Roy in a wave of emotion.

'You might be wondering,' Johnny Dexter began, his voice echoing off the back of the Tom Tully Stand, 'who is in charge?'

'Yes, boss,' some of the players said, as movement caught Roy's eye down the tunnel. Two figures, wearing Melchester Rovers strips. Who were they?

'Well,' Johnny went on, recovering Roy's attention. 'I'm in charge. With Frankie here. For now.'

'Where's Hamish?' Asif Mirza, the club's right back, asked.

'Gone.' Frankie Pepper stepped forward.

Roy glanced at Vic Guthrie and then Lofty Peak, team captain and vice-captain, to see if they knew anything. They would if anybody did. Lofty and Vic had blank, even confused, looks on their faces.

'People come. People go,' Johnny mused. 'That's football. We have to get used to change, whether we like it or not.'

That was true. Roy thought about his old friend – Blackie Gray – who'd just returned to Islington after a half-season loan. Then he noticed Johnny's eyes linger on him.

Roy stared back.

Johnny looked away quickly.

Now Roy was frowning. What was going on? Coach never looked away. He loved to stare out players, let them know who was boss.

'And on that subject,' Frankie Pepper interjected, 'we'd like to introduce you to two new players.'

Suddenly the squad was different. A murmur of voices. The pre-season lethargy and weariness evaporating. They were stretching their arms and legs, their eyes sharp. New players meant competition for places in the first team, a threat to existing players' careers. Roy felt it too: a rush of adrenaline. Or was it fear?

'Come on out, lads,' Frankie Pepper called down the tunnel.

Roy rubbed his chin. Change. Players come. Players go. He saw anxiety in his teammates' eyes as the two mystery men emerged from the shadows.

ONE OF THE two new players was tall and lean, with dark hair. Roy squinted, recognising him. Zhang. Zheng, maybe? He wasn't sure where he knew him from. The other was blond, stockier with a square jaw. Roy had never seen him before. But both were wearing Melchester Rovers' home tops and tracksuit bottoms, so he knew he would be seeing a lot more of them now.

New players?

It had never ever occurred to Roy they might be signing new players.

'Please meet Adey Winehouse and Zhang

Wei,' Frankie said. 'Wei has signed a season's deal and Adey is here for a couple of weeks' trial.'

Most of the existing squad were standing still, warily watching their new teammates, so Roy stepped forward and shook each player by the hand. Someone had to break the ice.

'I'm Roy Race,' he started. 'Welcome to Mel Park. I'm looking forward to playing with you this season. The rest of the lads will wake up soon.'

Now Vic Guthrie was right behind him. 'Vic Guthrie. Captain. I look forward to playing with you too. Did Roy mention, I'm the captain? And that I – for one – am going to be in the team this season.'

The whole squad was welcoming them now, a hubbub of voices. Roy maintained his smile as he wondered what on earth Vic had meant by that.

Who *wouldn't* be in the team this season?

TEN MINUTES LATER they were running. Out of the stadium and into the training pitches up the side of Mel Park. Led by Frankie Pepper.

'An easy one,' she called out. 'Chat while you run. Shout out what you did in the summer. I don't want you out of breath. That'll come soon enough.'

Several of the players mentioned holidays abroad. Bali. Florida. Australia.

'Roy?' Frankie Pepper asked. 'How about you?'

'France,' Roy replied. 'Went to watch the Women's World Cup.'

'Oooooh, women's football,' one of the group said, above the sound of studs clacking on concrete.

'Who was that?' Frankie Pepper turned to stare eighteen young men down, forcing them all to stop suddenly.

Silence.

No-one owning up.

'Well,' their physio said, 'if anyone

thinks that women playing football is funny, I'll take you on. Any of you? I am fitter, stronger and more skillful than everyone here. Agreed?'

Several voices agreed.

'I never want to hear that sort of old-fashioned attitude to the women's game again,' Frankie added firmly, a fury in her voice. 'Never. You really, *really* should be better than that.'

They ran on, cowed quiet, then stopped on the edge of the training pitch, players stooping to adjust their boot laces.

'Who did you go with, Roy?' Frankie asked Roy.

'My sister,' Roy said.

'And?'

'And his girlfriend... Vic's sister,' Gordon Stewart, the Rovers' keeper, added loudly.

'Yeah,' Roy said, glancing at Vic, who

was frowning. 'Ffion too.'

'Not happy about that, Vic?' Gordon laughed.

Vic looked up from straightening his shinpads. 'No,' he said. 'I really am not.'

As the Melchester Rovers' squad chuckled and the banter moved on, Roy glanced forward at his two new teammates.

That was when he noticed the number on the back of Adey Winehouse.

Nine.

He was wearing the number nine shirt. Roy felt so sick he could barely speak.

Roy checked Zhang Wei's number. It was eleven.

He jogged alongside Paco. From the wide-eyed look of shock on Paco's face, Roy knew he too had seen the numbers on the new players' backs.

'What's going on?' Paco asked, his voice

barely a whisper.

'We'll talk,' Roy said. 'After training.'

ROY AND PACO sprawled on the grass, drinking water to rehydrate after an hour working hard in the hot July sun.

'It's not right,' Paco fumed.

They had chosen to sit away from the others so that they could talk privately about the new players and the fact that Zhang was wearing eleven and Winehouse nine. The numbers Paco and Roy had wanted.

Roy could tell Paco would have a lot to say. He was hot-headed at times.

But, before they could get into it, a voice: 'I need to have a word with you two.'

Johnny Dexter stood over them, blocking the sun like a storm cloud. So far he had said nothing.

Paco couldn't hold himself back. 'What's going on, Coach? Our numbers?'

Coach frowned. His face was hard to read. He still looked like their don't-mess-with-me-Coach, but there was something else in his expression, something unreadable. Johnny Dexter was the straightest talker Roy knew. Honest. Blunt. Clear as a bell.

But not today.

Coach cleared his throat. 'I need... look lads... I...'

Definitely not today.

Roy and Paco sat in silence. They had no idea what to say to Coach. He was never like this. Roy opened his mouth to speak, but Coach put his hand on Paco's shoulder.

'You have to trust me,' Coach filled the

silence. 'You have to leave it with me and know that I am trying to do the right thing. And know... *know* that when I have something to tell you, I will tell you.'

'Okay...' Paco said, cautiously.

'And, until then, just go on as normal. You have... you have to trust me... I'm doing what I can...'

'About what?' Paco asked.

'I'm doing what I can...' Coach repeated.

'But I want to know why I am not number eleven,' Paco persisted. 'I want to know why there are secrets.'

Another silence.

Wanting to make things feel more comfortable, Roy spoke.

'We trust you one hundred per cent, Coach,' Roy said. 'Don't we, Paco?'

'Do we?' Paco was shaking his head.

'We do,' Roy eyed his friend. 'We have to.

Coach has always done the right thing by us.'

Roy looked at Paco, then at Johnny Dexter. The three of them said nothing.

Then Paco nodded. 'Okay,' he conceded. 'It's okay.'

'Thanks lads,' Coach said, turning to leave.

'I don't understand,' Paco whispered to Roy when he had gone.

'Nor me, mate,' Roy said. 'But all we can do is believe in Coach. He's the one man we can trust. Hasn't he always been straight with us?'

Paco sighed. 'It is true. Okay. For now.'

'Now then lads,' Coach called the players back together. 'Time for some more running. Then, the big reveal...'

'What?' Duncan McKay asked.

'You'll see.'

Roy saw Coach manage a faint smile.

'GATHER ROUND, LADS,' Coach said.

Roy and his teammates walked, some with hands on hips, to the centre circle where Johnny Dexter and Frankie Pepper stood, waiting to speak to them.

Frankie handed out bottles of water.

'Rehydrate,' she ordered. 'Look at the state of you. You've only run two miles.'

Roy looked around at his teammates. Most were soaked in sweat.

'Water out: water in,' Frankie said. 'Your muscles will cramp if you don't keep hydrated.'

Once the team were sitting on the floor, several of them stretching out their muscles after their workout, Coach faced them and smiled.

'Time for the big reveal,' he said.

'What?' Vic Guthrie joked. 'Why Roy's not wearing nine this season?'

The laughter that started after Vic's remark faded rapidly as the other players noticed Coach's reaction.

Johnny Dexter had said nothing, his eyes on the ground. Roy watched his chest rise and fall. Silence descended on the group. Vic went from looking cocky to sheepish: they all knew he'd said something wrong, just not what it was. And Roy knew he was at the centre of it.

Just what was going on?

'Our pre-season tour,' Coach said, ignoring the weird atmosphere.

Several players leaned forward. They wanted to know where they were going on tour. It was their first time on a club tour. They were excited. They knew it might involve travelling abroad.

'Tromsø,' Coach said.

'Bless you,' Gordon Stewart joked.

Coach waited for the laughter to die down, shaking his head, but smiling now.

'Tromsø, gents, is a town in Norway. Its second best team is called Tromsdalen. They are hosting a Scandinavian tournament for teams from Norway, Sweden, Denmark and... us.'

'Any good?' Vernon Elliott asked.

'Yes and no,' Coach said enigmatically.

'So... why... us?'

'Why do several Scandinavian teams want to play us?'

'Yeah.'

'Because of this badge, lads,' Coach purred, holding the front of his training vest out by the Melchester Rovers badge. 'You must not forget... we are Melchester Rovers. We are the stuff of legend. You can forget your Citys and your Uniteds. Out there – in the slightly... older generations – are thousands of Scandinavian Melchester Rovers fans. They love us. When I was a player we had Norwegians and Swedes coming to every game at Mel Park. Fine people. We are sure to have a good time.'

'Will it be cold?' Patrick Nolan, the Irish Under-19 striker, asked.

Johnny Dexter studied his team. 'Tromsø is the most northern football town in the world. It's in the Arctic, Patrick. For one third of the year the sun doesn't even rise. So – yes – it is cold. But now? Not so much. I'd say 15 degrees. Pretty mild for the Arctic.'

'What's the plan, boss?' Roy asked, after watching his teammates muttering to each other in twos and threes.

'Two semis. Then a final, or third place playoff.'

'How long do we have to get fit?' Vic Guthrie asked.

'No time.' Frankie Pepper started laughing.

'Eh?'

'What Frankie means is…' Coach said, 'we leave tomorrow. Flying from Melchester.'

Now there was noise. Several conversations all going on at once. Complaints. Groans. But excitement too.

'Beats running, running, running,' Vernon Elliott said.

'Maybe…' Frankie Pepper replied.

'We won't be running when we're there, will we?' Vernon asked, cautious.

Frankie did not reply.

Tomorrow? Roy stared at his feet. He was excited to be going on a pre-season tour. And abroad. But tomorrow? He felt a deep-down unease. For a moment the wasn't sure what it was about, his thoughts all foggy.

He was thinking about the other parts of his life. His dad. Ffion. Everything not football.

His dad had been ill for months now. A brain tumour. An operation that half-paralysed and shut off most of his speech. They'd coped as a family, however hard it had been. But recently Dad had not been quite right. Roy wasn't sure what it was, but all the progress he'd made had stopped.

And then there was Ffion. In France, Roy and Ffion had talked a lot. They'd got to know each other. It was a weird feeling, but Roy realised that he'd miss her when he was away. But the most pressing issue was that he'd promised to go to the cinema with her tomorrow. And now he couldn't. He'd have to tell her couldn't make it when he went to see her team training tonight.

So, although going to Norway to play football was good, there were some things Roy didn't want to leave behind.

6

Roy was a few minutes late when he arrived at the sports centre on the edge of town. He knew that the girls had already started from the sound of the thud of balls against the cage that surrounded the outdoor pitches and by the shouts of the players.

He turned the corner to see a group of footballers training as hard as he'd ever seen any team train before. Far harder than his League One squad. He stood at a slight distance and watched.

Ffion Guthrie was standing at the head of two rows of Sowerby FC players, who were passing the ball hard and fast to each other on the 3G pitches, then sprinting round to the end of the row, where bright yellow and orange cones had been set out. It was intense stuff. Even though the day had clouded over it was still hot and – as he got closer – Roy saw the players were breathing hard, sweat pouring off them.

Ffion looked across at Roy for a second, but remained focussed on the drill, shouting out to her players to keep it up. To go faster.

Roy watched his sister – Rocky – among them, working extra hard. Annoying though she was, Roy admired his sister. Even in drills, simple skill sessions, anything, she would work so hard that she was shattered once finished. If she wanted something she would give it everything: and Roy knew she wanted football. A year ago she didn't even have a school team to play in. Now, things were different. Now she was in a team, and was galvanised by England doing so well in the World Cup finals in France.

After the drill, Ffion led the team in two laps of the pitch, slowing them down until they were jogging, breathing slowly and deeply, most of them smiling.

'Right. Stretches,' Ffion ordered. 'A full set of tens,' she called out and the Sowerby squad hit the floor.

Press ups.

Squat thrusts.

Burpees.

Roy watched, smiling. They looked fit. They looked so fit and strong. Far more than a few months ago. He was looking at a different sort of team. Hard-working, serious, focussed. Every one of them. All led by Ffion Guthrie. His girlfriend.

Roy felt a rush of pride.

This team needed to be fit. Strong too. In less than a week's time they had a game. A game that could change everything for them; that, if they won, they would be in a league competition that was at the foot of the pyramid leading all the way up to the Women's Premier League.

Roy waited at the side of the pitch, leaning against the fence as Ffion went round all the players, back-slapping and encouraging.

Thanking them. She was a hell of a coach. A leader. Roy liked that about her. And unlike her brother, Vic, she never let her guard slip. She was never mean or selfish.

As the players filed past Roy, a couple nodding hello to him and Rocky fired a shot out of her water bottle, soaking Roy's shirt.

'Funny,' Roy shouted.

'It was. I know,' Rocky replied to an outburst of laughter from her teammates.

Then Ffion.

She looked at his Melchester Rovers tracksuit top. 'Thought I might see you in a Tynecaster top?' she muttered.

'What?' Roy felt a flash of anger and tried to hide it.

He failed.

'Just a joke,' Ffion smiled, hand on his arm. 'What is it, Roy?' she asked, looking at him through slightly narrowed eyes.

'What do you mean?' Roy asked.

Ffion squinted and brushed the front of Roy's top.

'There's something up,' she said. 'With you.'

Roy screwed up his face. 'How did you know?'

'I'm clever,' Ffion said. 'And I can read you like a matchday programme.'

'Well... I... er... can't go to the cinema tomorrow.'

'I see,' Ffion said.

Roy watched her shoulders drop slightly. He was kind of pleased to see she was disappointed. He went to put his arm round her.

'Why?' Ffion stepped away. 'And let's not do that hand-holding stuff in front of the girls, eh?'

Roy understood. 'Sorry,' he said.

Ffion smiled, her eyes staring deep into his. 'Even though I'd like to. I'm Coach to this lot. I want it to stay simple.'

'Understood,' Roy said.

'Anyway,' Ffion changed the subject. 'Why are you standing me up?'

'Well…' Roy replied. 'I'm going to the Arctic. I'm sorry.'

'Really?' Now Ffion sounded excited.

'Really.'

'With?'

'Rovers.'

Ffion nodded. 'When?' she asked.

'In twelve hours.'

Ffion started laughing.

'What?' Roy was never sure what Ffion's laughter meant. They'd been going out for a few weeks. But he still felt unsure whether she liked him.

She put her hand on his shoulder again.

'You like to keep me on my toes, don't you?' she smiled. 'One minute we're going to see a film, then next you're an Arctic explorer.'

'It's a pre-season tournament,' Roy explained. 'In a city called Tromsø. Right up in the north of Norway. I think we have to get there by boat or something.'

Ffion nodded. It was clear she was disappointed. Roy felt guilty that he'd sounded so excited telling her the details. They walked alongside each other, not speaking. He felt the impulse to take her hand, but stopped himself. She'd asked him not to. It was fine. But Roy wondered what she was thinking. There were so many things he still didn't understand about her, about them. This silence was one of them.

What should he say now?

And then he had an idea. Her match.

She'd be thinking about her match in a week's time. It meant so much to her. And she might be worried.

'We'll be back for your match,' Roy said. 'We fly in that afternoon.'

Roy watched Ffion's frown melt away, her eyes on his.

'You promise?' she said.

'Yeah,' Roy said. 'I'm there.'

'You'd better be,' Ffion said. 'I need your eyes on the game. I'll be playing.'

And Roy swore to himself: even if he had to swim across the North Sea, he'd be there for Ffion.

INTERNATIONAL DEPARTURES, MELCHESTER Airport. Bright lights, long corridors, huge windows with views of aircraft being refuelled and resupplied.

It was ten in the morning. Aware he was running late, Roy wheeled his dad's chair, weaving between groups of holidaymakers with large roller suitcases. Mum alongside them. They'd come on the bus. It was free for Dad and one other. Much cheaper than a taxi.

Roy quickly identified the rest of the Rovers' squad – their red and yellow tracksuits picking them out from the other travellers. He could hear them too. Laughing. Shouting. Winding each other up.

A sudden silence fell when Roy showed up pushing his dad's wheelchair. Roy wished it didn't happen, but it often did. People thought they had to stop laughing – just being normal – when someone in a wheelchair showed up.

Johnny Dexter pushed his hand through his hair and called out: 'Danny. Mrs Race. It's good to see you both,' trying to mask the uneasy silence. 'This – lads – is one of the greatest supporters our football club has ever had. I want you to shake his hand.'

Vic Guthrie led the players to shake Dad's hand, then Mum's.

Roy couldn't but smile as Coach squatted to talk eye to eye with Dad. Coach was right about Dad: he had once been president of the supporters' club. He was the number one fan when Coach and Rovers were among the greatest in Europe.

But times had changed.

On and off the field.

Roy was too bothered about his dad to worry why the rest of his teammates had gone quiet when he appeared in his wheelchair. Bothered, because of how his dad had been this morning. His eyes had been a bit more bloodshot, like when he'd first been ill. And he wasn't taking everything in, his concentration fading in and out.

Roy looked at Mum as the two men talked. Mum stared back, a blank expression fixed on her face. Roy knew she was concerned too, but that she didn't want it affecting Roy's football.

'Have a great time, Roy,' she said.

'Do you want me to stay?' Roy asked.

'Stay? Why?'

'Dad,' Roy muttered.

Mum lowered her head, then fixed her eyes back on her son.

'You have work to do,' she told him. 'This is your job. You're living your dream. And Dad's fine.'

'He's not. I can tell. Something's going on.'

'I can cope. I've got Rocky.'

'I want to stay,' Roy insisted.

Mum shook her head. 'Think on, Roy Race,' she said. 'You told me last night that someone else has got the number nine shirt and that you want it. We need your income. You bring in £800 a week playing for Rovers. Without it we're stuffed. I need you to work. I need you on that plane fighting for your place, not moping around with us at home. Do you understand me?'

Roy glanced at Gordon Stewart and Duncan MacKay, who were watching this mother-son exchange.

Duncan wagged his finger at Roy. Roy smiled back at them and rolled his eyes.

'Do you?' Mum repeated.

'Yes, Mum. I'm on it.'

Frankie Pepper had appeared now. She was handing out passports and boarding cards. Roy took his chance to say goodbye to his dad, kneeling next to him.

Johnny Dexter stood up, putting his hand on Roy's shoulder, squeezing slightly. Then he was gone, telling Vernon Elliott to get off his phone and that he'd dropped his boarding card.

'Look after Mum while I'm away,' Roy said to Dad.

Dad smiled.

'What shall I bring you back from the Arctic?' Roy asked.

Dad shrugged. Another smile. His eyes were even redder than they'd been that morning. Roy felt a ripple of panic pass through him. But he didn't want his dad to notice.

'A reindeer?' he joked.

Dad smiled again.

'A glacier?' Roy tried again.

Dad said nothing. Roy was hoping this would be one of those rare moments – once-a-week moments – where Dad said one word that made a massive difference. Like when he'd said 'Go' when Roy was wondering whether to crash the Melchester Rovers' trial last season. Or 'Stupid' when Roy wasn't making the right choices. Words Roy would remember for the rest of his life.

But Dad was silent. He broke their gaze, so Roy stood up. His ripple of panic had become a tsunami of fear. What if Dad got worse this week? What if...

Roy stopped himself thinking and remembered what his mum had just said. She needed his money. She needed him to be focussed. With that, Roy grabbed Dad round the shoulders and hugged him fiercely. Roy would work harder on his football this year, more than he ever had before. He'd make sure his parents were okay.

'I'll score you a goal. An Arctic goal. How about that?'

Dad nodded.

Now Roy just had to keep his promise.

8

THE PLANE TOUCHED down in Tromsø at midnight, following delays to the team's connecting flight from Oslo. As instructed, the whole squad stayed in their seats even when the seatbelt lights flickered off.

Roy took the chance to text Ffion.

Landed. It's light at midnight. x

A reply came back immediately.

Must be good. It's made you all poetic. xx

'I don't get it,' Vic Guthrie said, peering out through the window.

'Get what?' Asif Mirza asked.

'Is it midnight at home? But, like… not midnight here?' Vic sounded confused. 'I mean. It's still light. What's going on?'

Johnny Dexter was on his feet, making sure his players continued to let all of the other passengers off the plane first.

'You've not done your homework, have you, Vic?' he laughed. 'We're in the Arctic Circle now. The sun hasn't set for eight weeks. And won't for another month. It doesn't. Not in summer.'

Roy watched Vic's face crumple as he tried to work it out.

'And that's not your last surprise, either,' Coach smiled, peering out at one of the windows at the terminal building. Then he said quietly, almost to himself, 'Not if

I remember what happened the last time Melchester Rovers came to Scandinavia.'

OUTSIDE IT WAS warm, for midnight. Around them – beyond the flat lands of the runway and nearby fields – was a ring of mountains that appeared blue in the half-light of the Arctic midnight. There was a cool wind blowing from the north, ruffling the players' hair.

'This is crazy,' Vernon Elliott said, stopping to look at the views. 'It's warm and cold at the same time. It's light, but dark. I don't understand.'

They walked across the tarmac, turning to stare as a freight plane fired its engines, thundered down the runway, then took off, its roaring fading into the Arctic night.

Then another sound, only audible now

the freight plane had gone. A weird noise like a small football crowd. Roy wondered if there was a stadium nearby, or if there was some sort of midnight league. Surely not.

'Do you hear that?' Roy asked Adey Winehouse.

Adey nodded. 'Something. What is it?'

Roy shrugged, as the automatic doors to the airport terminal building opened and the Melchester squad were hit by a wall of noise. At least a couple of hundred women, men and children, all wearing Melchester Rovers shirts and scarves, were waiting on the other side of the customs and passport control.

Coach stopped the players and Frankie Pepper handed out their passports.

'In my day,' Coach mused, his chest sticking out, 'I had letters from kids every week from cities like Stockholm, Oslo and Copenhagen. Those boys and girls,' he pointed. 'That's them. With their own daughters and sons now. A generation on. These are the club's fans. And I know you're all tired, but I want you to give them all the time they need. They're out here way past their bedtime. That includes the adults. So let's show them how grateful we are for this reception.'

AFTER HALF AN hour of meeting and greeting two generations of Scandinavian Melchester Rovers fans, Roy was exhausted. It had been a long day. He joined his teammates on a bus that was going to take them to their hotel in the centre of Tromsø, the grin on his face aching.

He was overwhelmed.

What lovely people. All of them.

He had almost been moved to tears when

a pair of twins asked for a photo with him, both of them in that season's top, both of them with the word RACE above a number fourteen, his number last season.

'Right lads,' Johnny Dexter said. 'It's a short drive into town. Straight to bed. We've got an early start and another surprise for you in the morning.'

'What surprise?' Paco Diaz asked, suspiciously.

'Wait. And. See,' Frankie Pepper said, smirking at Johnny Dexter.

THEY MET IN the hotel foyer, by the reception desk, all of them wearing Melchester Rovers tracksuits. Roy arrived with Lofty Peak, who he was sharing a room with. Both of them felt funny. Roy reckoned it was something to do with the fact it hadn't gone dark last night. He felt like he'd hardly slept.

Frankie Pepper checked each players' footwear and Patrick Nolan and Lofty were sent back to their rooms to change.

'You'll need something more sturdy than those,' Frankie laughed.

Roy wondered what she was laughing

about, what this surprise was that Coach had mentioned the night before. Why did they need sturdy footwear?

He took the time to text Rocky.

How's Dad? Mum?

Okay.

Is he any better?

Same.

Roy bristled. His sister was the master of the one-word text. He wished she could give him a bit more.

They walked through Tromsø, a beautiful wood-built town surrounded by clear water and mountains, over a bridge to the foot of a hill where a steep winding path led at least four hundred meters upwards, next to a cable car to take tourists to the top without the pain of the climb.

'Thankfully...' Lofty Peak said loudly. 'There's a cable car.'

Roy felt disappointed. He had a bit of a thing about hills. He wanted to climb it. Even run it. Just to see if he could.

'I agree,' Coach said from the rear. 'That's how me and Frankie are travelling. You lot? A bit of leg-strength work. There's a nice café at the top. We'll meet you up there. I'll stand you a glass of water.'

There were moans of complaint.

'Or do you fancy doing running all day again?' Frankie threatened.

Every member of the team moved towards the start of the path without another word. They would walk. Anything was better than running.

*   *   *

THE ENTIRE MELCHESTER Rovers first team arrived at the top of the hill and looked down to see Tromsdalen and Tromsø below, divided by a stretch of water with a white bridge that looked like a shard of ice floating on the fjord. The town appeared small now, set against a backdrop of wilderness and mountain ranges.

After a drink and some stretching with Frankie, Coach told them his plan.

'We're going to hike across the tops and drop down into a fjord, then head on towards the west. This is about strong legs. Heart rate. We'll do some ball-work later. This is also about team building. Your aim is to have some sort of conversation with every other member of the squad before we get back. Understood?'

'Understood,' said some of the players.

'If any of you fancy a bit of cryotherapy, all you need to do is take a dip in the fjord when we come back down.'

Coach surveyed the sky. 'Have a good drink of water before we set off. And take one bottle each. We've a long hike before lunchtime.'

They walked.

And walked.

Roy started out with Adey Winehouse. Then Zhang Wei. He made sure he talked to Patrick Nolan for a good few minutes too. Even though Nolan was quiet, Roy knew they had to be close, especially now that Blackie Gray – Roy's former striking partner – was back at Islington. If Roy and Patrick were to be partners they had to be comfortable with each other. Team building, Coach had said.

It was when Roy found himself alone, gazing at the fjords, that Coach butted in.

'Roy?'

'Coach?'

'I feel bad, Race.'

Roy frowned. 'Do you need some water, Coach?' Roy offered Coach his bottle.

Johnny Dexter laughed. 'No. Bad about you. Bad about us. Not bad... you know.'

Roy decided to say nothing. He really *didn't* know. This must be about what had happened two days before, back at Mel Park. All the mysterious things Coach had been trying to explain to Roy and Paco. Or not.

'Can I tell you a story?' Coach asked. 'It's... well... it's about a mate of mine. At another club. It'll help explain what I want to say to you.'

'Fine, boss,' Roy agreed.

'So... my mate's a manager at – let's say – a League Two outfit,' Coach started. 'He's got this player on his books. A nice lad. The best player in his squad. Worth more than all the other players put together. A fantastic future. You know the type?'

Roy nodded. 'I think so, boss.'

'So, the chairman at the club wants to sell this striker, because he is short-sighted and greedy. And a winger at the club as well. To a top-flight team. The chairman wants to cash in. And my mate – the manager – gets told this.'

Roy frowned. What was this?

'But also – and this is the important bit, Race – he is told that he cannot tell the player what the plans are and that if he does he'll be sacked. And – even though he is desperate to be honest with this boy, who has always been honest with him, and wants the boy to know that there is no way he's going to let the chairman sell him, to the point he would quit and leave the club himself – he can't.'

'That sounds tough for your mate,' Roy said, glancing at Coach, just as they hit a bit of rough ground, scattered rocks, scree.

'Ow,' Roy winced, as he lost his balance and had to grab Coach to stop himself falling.

'Twist?' Coach asked him.

'Just a little one. Nothing serious.'

'Sure?'

Roy bounced on his ankles, testing them, and smiled at Coach. 'No problem, Gaffer.'

'So, do we understand each other, Race?' Coach asked.

'Yeah, course we do, Coach,' Roy said, still trying to work out what Coach was going on about.

10

AFTER THE HIKE and some ball work, the team had had an early night and were fully refreshed for day two in Tromsø.

And for game one. The day Roy would begin the fight to win his place back in the Melchester Rovers team.

They walked across the bridge as a large red and white cruise ship was sailing up the fjord beneath them and on to the Tuil Stadium, Tromsdalen.

Roy was last into the dressing room. He was last in because he'd been staring in awe at the ring of mountains that surrounded the stadium. It was spectacular. And the sky was clear. It was so clear he could see a larger mountain range in the distance, snow-capped peaks in July.

He felt an urge to run up the mountains again. He had so much in his head. What Coach had said. The texts from Rocky. But not now. Not yet.

What came next would happen in the Tuil Stadium, a small stadium with one main stand that would seat about two thousand, with smaller stands around the other three sides of the pitch.

Time to focus.

Time for the game.

Time to forget mountains, fjords and snow-capped peaks.

Because Roy was last in, every other player had seen the team sheet ahead of him: pinned on the wall of the away dressing room. Roy stood at the back trying to see his name. He caught a few glances from team mates. Lofty Peak gave him a sympathetic look.

Bad sign.

It was only when Paco turned round that Roy knew that he wasn't in the team.

'We're both subs,' Paco mumbled.

Roy was stunned. He felt sick.

'I reckon you're toast, Roy,' laughed Vic, ruffling Roy's hair as he shouldered past. 'Coach probably doesn't think you can make the step up to League One. You need a bit more character, maybe? With a bit of luck, my sister might dump you too. Ha!'

Roy noticed Duncan MacKay and Gordon Stewart laugh at Vic's joke.

'Not the case,' Johnny Dexter's deep voice drowned out the others. 'We're going narrow today and Roy turned his ankle on the hike yesterday.'

'Narrow?' Paco complained. 'Melchester Rovers? We are all about wing play.'

'I'm the boss,' Coach said, sounding cross that Paco was challenging him again. 'We go narrow first half. I might deploy you second, Diaz. But not if you give me any more of that backchat, thank you.'

The players put on their kits in silence.

Roy looked around at his teammates as they dressed. Some of them caught his eye; some of them avoided it.

He felt miserable.

IT WAS IMPOSSIBLE to feel miserable once the game had started.

The noise from the small crowd was fantastic. Roy estimated there were 500 Tromsdalen FC fans, wearing red and blue tops and scarves. But he saw 500 or more in Melchester red and yellow. All chanting songs together. Roy recognised one of the songs by The Beatles, but he wasn't sure which. There were fans from Sweden and Denmark too. A party atmosphere. And – next to the players' tunnel – a slim sliver and gold trophy, about half a meter high. It glistened in the Arctic sun.

Roy wanted it. Like he wanted every trophy he saw.

As the players lined up for kick off, Johnny Dexter sat next to Roy on the bench. Roy looked at him.

'What?' Coach asked, grumpily. 'You got a question?'

'No,' Roy said quickly. Then, 'Yes. Yes, I do.'

'Spit it out.' Dexter's eyes were back on the pitch.

'Why?' Roy asked.

'Your ankle,' Coach replied. 'Like I said. I dropped you because you turned your ankle. I was walking right next to you, remember?'

'No,' Roy shook his head. 'Not my ankle. I've accepted that. I want to know why are these fans so into Melchester Rovers?'

Coach beamed. 'We used to be the best-supported team in Norway,' he said, his voice mild, mellifluous. 'They've not forgotten. After all these years. After our... decline. They still love us, Roy.'

AT HALF TIME Roy could sense that, although the Norwegian Melchester fans might have been excited by Rovers being in town, they were *not* excited by the team's performance.

The team's narrow formation couldn't cope with the pressing game of Tromsdalen. The Melchester forwards weren't getting any ball – and, when they did, they were squandering it. The striking duo of the trialist, Winehouse, and Patrick Nolan wasn't working. At all.

By half time it was 2-0 to the home side. And, minutes into the second half, 3-0.

Roy breathed out. He was torn. On the one hand, he wanted Melchester Rovers to win: on the other, he wanted the team to miss *him*. Roy hated feeling like this. But he couldn't deny that a part of him was pleased Rovers weren't as a good a team when he was on the bench.

Coach stared at the floor when the third goal went in and muttered something. Roy didn't catch it word for word, but he knew Coach was unhappy.

Then the crowd chanting changed.

A new chant.

Roy couldn't make out what they were chanting. He looked at the Tromsdalen bench to see if one of their players was warming up. Maybe they'd left one of their key players on the bench too?

Coach sighed as they both watched Adey Winehouse trip over the ball. He was still having a bad game. Like Nolan. Johnny Dexter sighed again. Then let out a dark laugh.

'I hate this,' Coach volunteered. 'I hate this job. I can't wait for Mouse to come back. Roy? This being a manager lark... it's not for me.'

Roy turned to face Johnny Dexter. 'Coach?'

'You heard what they're calling?'

Roy was about to say no - but then it clicked.

'Oh... They're saying...'

'They're saying we want Race. Roy Race,' Coach said. 'Warm up.'

'What about my ankle?' Roy asked.

'Your ankle... it's fine. Just... just... warm up, will you? And I want you on the left wing. Not down the middle. Let's just be safe, yeah? You too, Paco.' Coach leaned over to speak to Diaz. 'Warm up. I want you on the other wing. I don't care what... ah... forget it...'

Roy didn't need telling a third time. He jogged out with Paco to the roar of the small crowd, noticing Johnny Dexter having a quiet word with the Tromsdalen coach. Roy wondered what Coach would want to say to his opposite number. But – as soon as he was warming up – all thoughts other than football faded from his mind.

He was going on.

This was his chance. Even if he was on the wing.

And once he was on the pitch and over the line, there was only football.

ROY DECIDED TO enjoy playing on the wing. He didn't get the chance often. And – after scoring goals – he loved nothing more than running at defenders, trying to avoid tackles. There was a freedom on the wing that you didn't have as a striker. It was more creative, if you wanted it to be.

He was pleased that Adey Winehouse was happy to play him in. Adey was one of those forwards who would take the ball with his back to the defence, hold it strong, then play it out wide before pushing forward.

Not unlike Roy, really. But Roy wasn't going to worry about that. Not yet.

Adey was not starving Roy of the ball. He was giving it to him every time. He was being a team player. That was the best way to be. There was no way Roy was going to be selfish and exclude Adey. This was a team game. They were three down. It was time to do something about it.

Together.

Roy positioned himself to Adey's right, making himself the obvious pass. Then he would attack. Hard and fast. Down the line. Not wasting a second to give the Norwegians a chance to rein him in.

It took three or four attacks, Patrick Nolan missing two decent headers from Roy's crosses, before Roy started to wonder what was going on.

What was it? The thing that was going on?

It was too easy. That was it.

But not easy like Tromsdalen weren't a good side. They were. That's why they were 3-0 ahead.

The problem was something else.

It was too easy because none of the opposition players were tackling him. They would try to guide him wide, into the corners, but they never tried to take the ball.

Really?

That couldn't be true. Could it?

Roy decided to test his theory. To take a risk.

The next time Adey pinged the ball out to him, Roy ran directly at the goal. Not down the wing. Not round the back to loop a cross in. Just head-on towards goal. Roy advanced, showing as much of the ball as he dared to the defenders, trying to draw a tackle. He powered past Vic Guthrie. Suddenly he was on the edge of the box, untackled. It was like playing FIFA against one of those teams that don't challenge.

In on goal now, powering into the box, Roy unleashed a screamer.

The Tromsdalen keeper didn't move. Just stood there as the ball whizzed past him and almost burst the net.

Goal.

3-1.

The kind of strike that a player could boast about for weeks. That a player could pin onto his Twitter account. If he still had one.

But – to Roy, even though he'd scored the goal he had promised his dad he would score – the goal didn't feel right. It was like they'd let him score.

He didn't celebrate properly. He just jogged up to the Melchester fans and applauded them, turned to thank Adey Winehouse for the pass.

Then he spoke to Vic Guthrie. 'They're not tackling me,' he complained.

Vic scratched his head. 'I know,' he mused. 'I almost tried myself.'

Roy smiled. That was quite funny. For Vic.

'But why?' Roy asked.

12

Vic shrugged. He was holding the ball after the Tromsdalen keeper had lobbed it out.

'Why is no-one tackling you, Race?' he replied. 'I don't care. Just keep running at them like that. We could get a draw if you net two more. Then it's penalties. Stop thinking. Start playing.'

Vic handed Roy the ball.

Roy jogged back to the centre circle, then took up his place for the kick-off. Vic was right. They were on the pitch. Nothing else mattered but goals. The whats and whys and whos were meaningless. Until the final whistle at least.

Chasing the game, taking risks, Melchester were playing four up front now. Nolan and Winehouse in the middle. Diaz on the left, Roy on the right wing. And, as the Tromsdalen players backed off, keen to keep their lead, the wingers took flight.

With twenty minutes to go Roy carved up the right at speed, then glanced up to find neither striker in a good position. But Paco was, wide on the left.

Roy unleashed a powerful crossfield ball that bounced once before Paco trapped it, looked up, then began waltzing along the touchline, playing in Winehouse, who backed into a defender, and side-footed it to Nolan on the six yard line.

Nolan hit it. The ball cannoned off the keeper, back to Roy, just as Winehouse drew the last defender away, giving Roy all the room he needed to fire the ball into the roof of the net. The keeper, still on the floor after his save, had no chance.

GOAL!

3-2.

There was hope now. Real hope.

Adey Winehouse was in the back of the net, grabbing the ball to put it on the centre spot. Roy ran alongside him, trying to talk above the noise of the crowd who were galvanised now.

'You're doing great, Adey. Well done.'

Adey looked surprised. 'Th… thanks Roy. That means a lot.'

Then Roy realised something. Something obvious.

Adey Winehouse looked up to him. He wasn't after his place in the team. He was an eager young footballer at the beginning of his career. He needed support. And Roy was determined to give it to him.

But time was running out.

Fifteen minutes to go.

Then, in a flash, ten minutes.

Melchester were making chances. But they had yet to find an equaliser to take the game to penalties – and win this semi-final. There was a trophy to be won. They needed a piece of luck.

And still Roy hadn't been tackled. So, with time running out, he took to running into the penalty area. If he could get a shot on target, or play in Adey or Patrick, they'd have a chance. Roy knew you had to make your own luck.

And that's what happened.

A tackle on Roy at last.

A bad one. In the area.

Just as Roy was about to hit the ball – from a perfectly weighted Winehouse pass

– and complete his hat trick, a leg came in from nowhere and he was down, twisting his knee as he fell.

The referee's whistle silenced the roars of the crowd.

Adey helped Roy up. He handed Roy the ball.

Roy shook his head and put the ball back in Adey's hands. 'You take it,' Roy said.

Adey shook his head. 'Your hat trick?'

Roy shrugged.

'You deserve one.'

Roy saw Adey Winehouse's face break out into a grin, then he stepped back behind the eighteen-yard line to allow the trialist to place the ball on the spot and step back.

Roy gazed around the stadium. The eager fans. The range of mountains around them. He felt good. He was happy. It was always like this: whatever his worries off the pitch, once he was playing football nothing else mattered.

So, Adey Winehouse stepped up to equalise and take the game to penalties… and fired it over the bar.

The trialist squatted on the ground, his head in his hands. Roy jogged over to him.

'Stand up, Adey,' Roy said.

Adey stood and peered into Roy's eyes. He looked devastated.

Roy struggled to find the right thing to say. This was a massive moment in the youngster's career. He had to get it right.

'You'll not be judged on missing a penalty,' Roy said calmly. 'You'll be judged on how you react after missing it. I know. I've done worse. Much worse. This is not the end: it's the beginning.'

*   *   *

ONCE THE FINAL whistle went and the Melchester Rovers players had applauded the Tromsdalen team off their own pitch after a 3-2 defeat, Roy realised he needed time to himself. He liked sharing a room with Lofty Peak. They were mates. But Roy was used to time on his own. Now was one of those times.

He needed to get away from everyone. And from football. Just for a while.

TIME ON YOUR own. It's easier to think when you're on your own. So – after a dinner with players from all four teams taking part in the tournament – Roy drifted away from all the others and headed up the mountain. He told Frankie what he was doing. He knew she'd want to know. But also that she wouldn't stop him.

On foot.

It was steep and hard work, but, as soon as he was alone and away from buildings and roads, he could feel his mind relax amid the trees and grass. The sky was pale but still light with clouds drifting above him.

Half way up his phone pinged.

You okay? F x

Up a mountain. Need space.

Be careful. It's nearly dark.

Not here.

Oh yeah… I miss you.

Me you xx

Roy put his phone away and carried on walking. Like he'd said to Ffion: he needed space. It was good for him. He did it at home. If things with Dad became too much, he'd just head for the Moor and the woods. Up the mountain things felt good. For a while. But then the thoughts he'd not had a chance to explore all week came to him faster and faster.

Questions. Lots of questions.

And now... he didn't feel so good.

Why was Coach not playing him in the first eleven?

Why, when Coach did bring him on, did he put Roy out wide?

Was Adey Winehouse a threat?

Why had no-one tried to tackle him?

Was Vic right? Coach didn't think Roy could cut it in League One?

And then there was that story Coach had told him about that manager and his star player. He'd not even had time to think about that. But now he did.

The obvious question. Had Coach been talking about him? And Barry Cleaver?

And, if he was, did it mean something?

That couldn't be true. Could it? That Roy was going to be sold?

Roy scrambled on for another half hour, higher into the hills. The air was colder up here. A wind blowing southwards, directly from the North Pole. Roy smiled as he faced the wind and closed his eyes.

When he opened his eyes he saw a wide patch of snow ahead of him, still not melted by the summer sun. He sat down.

He tried to imagine what his dad would say to him if he was here – and if he could speak.

Roy scrambled on across scree and outcrops of hard grey rock, less and less vegetation. Tired after scrambling, he noticed something white moving about slowly. Roy hardly dared breathe as he watched what he thought might be a rabbit. Then he saw, by the way it was moving, it was a hare. An Arctic hare.

As he watched the hare, Roy thought again about his dad. About what he might say.

Dexter's always been a good guy. He's always been straight with you. Warned you when you've made mistakes. Praised you when you've needed it. But never too much.

Roy swallowed back the emotion swelling in his throat. That was just what Dad would say – and just the way he'd say it. He watched the hare lollop to another patch of greenery, looking back over its shoulder at Roy.

Trust him, Dad went on. *Trust him like you trust us. He's one hundred per cent Melchester and he cares a lot about you, Roy. If he's keeping something from you, there's a good reason. For you. For the club. Just trust him.*

Roy stood up. Dad was right.

Now the Arctic hare startled, scrambling in a wide arc away from him through scree and patches of snow and ice.

Roy sighed and stared at the huge sky around him. The glow of the sun from just below the horizon cast the mountains to the west as silhouettes. There was no sound now. The crack of stones under the hare's feet had stopped.

Roy looked down at his own feet. He

saw a stone, medium sized and brown, with threads of gold running though it. He picked it up. Something to give Ffion, he thought, smiling. He'd give her it when he saw her. It was the big game for Ffion and Rocky in two days, with kick-off at seven. Roy's plane landed at five. He'd be able to make it. If his plane was on time...

Roy looked around and listened to the wind. It was colder now. He felt alone and exposed. What if he fell? No-one would ever find him up here, even though he'd told Frankie where he was going. Time, he decided, to go back and join the others. They had a boat trip tomorrow. Then – the day after that – their second game. Against Swedish side Ornskoldsvik.

THE LOSERS' FINAL. Melchester Rovers versus Ornskoldsvik of Sweden.

Yesterday had been a rest day. They'd taken a boat trip out to see the fjords, then into the open sea. But today they were not tourists: today they were footballers.

Roy was warming up with a jog round the ground – after Johnny Dexter had told him he was on the bench again – when he saw a chauffeur-driven car pull up in the Tuil Stadium car park.

A familiar face climbed out. Alan Talbot. What was he doing here?

Roy pretended to do some stretching. But really he was watching Talbot. There was another man in the car too. It was hard to see who. But Roy did recognise the third man who walked over to join them.

Johnny Dexter.

What was Coach doing talking to Alan Talbot? Were they signing another new player?

Roy shook his head, then carried on

stretching. A few shuttle runs, building up to a faster and faster pace. More stretches. He was doing this because he wanted to be able to see what the three men were doing. He needed to know who the third man was.

Was he from another club?

Was he a player, even? Another striker? A better striker than Roy?

Eventually the man climbed out of the car, moving the seat so that Coach could get in, and Roy didn't have to wonder any longer.

The third man gazed over in the direction of Roy and grinned.

It was Barry Cleaver.

Roy was pretty sure that all the time he had been spying on the men grouped around the Aston Martin, Barry Cleaver had been spying on him.

With all three men in the car, it accelerated out of the car park, over the bridge and onto the mainland.

'Has he gone?'

Roy swung round, shocked so much he jumped. He had no idea who was behind him. Or how they could have got so close without him hearing.

'Yeah,' Roy replied.

'Good,' Frankie Pepper said. 'That means I'm in charge now. And that also means you're coming on a bit sooner than Coach planned. Like from kick off. Now.'

'Really?' Roy felt a smile widen on his face. 'Up front?'

Frankie Pepper shook her head. 'No can do, Race.' She frowned. 'Orders are Roy Race on the wing. And I don't want to see you in the penalty area. Got me?'

'Why?'

'Because orders are Roy Race has to stay out wide and not go in the box.'

'Yeah, but why?'

Frankie laughed. 'You don't ask why, Race,' she said. 'You do what you're told. You should be…'

'… grateful,' Roy interrupted. 'I know. But I still want to know why.'

'So do I, Race.' Frankie sounded exasperated. 'So do I.'

Roy lined up on the right wing. But, before kick off, he took the chance to have a conversation with the two strikers – Patrick Nolan and Adey Winehouse. If he wasn't going to be allowed in the penalty area, then he'd make sure they both were.

There was no way Melchester Rovers were going to lose this game.

THE ORNSKOLDSVIK PLAYERS were taller than all of the Melchester players, except Lofty Peak, who, in turn, towered above them.

'Play to feet,' Frankie shouted. 'Keep it on the ground. We've no chance if we go aerial.'

Roy was delighted. He loved to play football on the ground, so was happy to do as he was told.

With Melchester's first attack, Zhang Wei pinged the ball out to Roy on the wing. Roy took it in his stride and decided to test whether today was going to be a tackle-free day. He ran hard with the ball, inviting attempts to tackle.

A crunching foul flew in. Roy somersaulted, then leaped up to confront his Swedish counterpart, whose name, he could see, was Jansson.

To the Ornskoldsvik player's surprise, Roy put his hand out to shake.

'*Tack*, Jansson,' Roy said, using one of the few words he knew in Swedish. *Tack* meant thank you. The defender shook his hand, but didn't look any less confused. Why had this English player thanked him for fouling him?

Now, for Roy, the game felt real. Tackles. Fouls. Proper battles.

With the next attack, Duncan MacKay played the ball up the left, from the back. Roy took it and nutmegged the Swedish right winger, then he was away. Fast and hard, up the wing. He could hear the noise from the Norwegian Melchester fans as he ripped it up. Riding two reckless tackles, Roy reached the edge of the box and looked up to see Adey Winehouse sprinting into the penalty area. Having dragged the Swedish back four deep, Roy checked back and slid a pass in level with the penalty spot.

Adey Winehouse was onto it, side-footing it hard past the acrobatic dive of the keeper.

1-0.

Cheers erupted from the stands. And Roy felt good. He'd done the right thing. Played for the team, not for himself. It would still be 0-0 if he'd done that. He went over to congratulate Winehouse.

At the restart, Roy could see the fans sitting forward in their seats. This was the Melchester Rovers these fans had come to watch. And Roy didn't care if he was laying on goals or scoring them. He just wanted to be part of it.

As the game developed, Melchester took

more and more control, the Swedish defence backing off, intimidated by the fast-paced attacking style of the English team. Ten minutes after the first goal, Roy found himself running at Jansson again. As Roy tried to beat him, Jansson went to clip his ankle, but missed. And Roy was free. He lofted the ball to Zhang Wei, skirted the penalty area, took the return pass in a slick one-two, then volleyed the ball hard with his left foot.

The Rocket.

2-0.

Paco Diaz came on at half time. Zhang Wei went off, and Patrick Nolan gave way for a midfielder as Melchester switched to a four-three-three formation.

Now it was time to play Paco in. Get him on the goal scorer's sheet.

By the time the red Aston Martin returned to the Tuil Stadium, an hour into the game,

Melchester Rovers were thrashing the Swedes 4-0 and Roy was walking off, substituted and happy.

As he walked to the bench, he saw Johnny Dexter approaching him. Wanting to play it safe, Roy out his hand out to shake his Coach's hand. So he was surprised when Johnny Dexter grabbed him and folded him into a hard embrace.

'You okay, Coach?' Roy managed to say from inside the hug.

'I am not, Roy. I am not. But I know you are. You are more okay than I could ever dream and it's been an honour being your coach. I thank you.'

As Coach released Roy, Frankie Pepper jogged up to him.

'Good stuff, Race,' she said, hugging him too. 'And thanks for following orders.'

'My pleasure,' Roy replied. And it had

been. Roy felt better now about himself and his place at Melchester Rovers than he had throughout the rest of the close season.

Now he just wanted to get going in League One and see what Melchester Rovers could achieve at that level. Surely, there was no way they were going to get rid of him now?

16

FIVE P.M. THAT evening. Back at Melchester Airport.

Roy raced off the plane as soon as Coach allowed it, slaloming through groups of passengers who'd come off other flights and were working their way towards passport control.

He could make it.

If he was fast.

He did his best not to collide with anyone or to look too suspicious to the border police. There was no way he was going to let Rocky and Ffion down. Tonight was their decisive game, the game of their lives. If they won they would be in the pyramid. If not, they'd have to wait another year. He was desperate for them to succeed.

And Ffion had said she wanted him there.

Rocky had not said so herself, but Roy wanted to be there for her too, whether she did or not.

Roy dodged under several of the barriers at passport control, pushing in front of other people, saying 'Sorry... sorry... I have to go and see my sister.'

He knew he sounded like a lunatic. But sometimes it doesn't matter what strangers think of you: it matters what the people you love think of you. So long as you weren't rude. So long as you said you were sorry.

As he queued for his passport to be checked he looked inside his rucksack to make sure the present he'd brought for Ffion was still there. It was, wrapped in a small square gift box that Roy had bought at the airport. Roy grinned at the thought of giving it to her.

The woman at passport control looked at his passport, then his face.

'Roy Race?' she asked. 'Where have you travelled from?'

'Er...' Roy's mind was blank. This was terrible. He was so focussed on what was happening next that he had forgotten what had happened before.

'I... I can't remember,' he spluttered.

The woman smiled, covering her mouth with her hand.

'You've been to Norway, Mr Race,' she said. 'You scored a Rocket against Ornskoldsvik this lunchtime. Am I right?'

Roy nodded, recovering a little. 'Yes. Thank you. Brain freeze. That's the Arctic for you.'

The woman laughed again and handed him his passport. 'Good luck this season, Roy. I'm a Tom Tully Stand season ticket holder and – just so you know – we love you. And we don't believe a word of it.'

Roy gave her a quizzical look. What was that comment about? Before he could worry about it too much, he remembered the rush

he was in and sprinted away.

Roy slowed down again to pass calmly through customs. You didn't run through customs. You didn't sweat through customs. You looked calm. You looked like a good citizen. Then they wouldn't want to look through your bag.

Once through passports and customs – channelled through a set of metallic doors that snapped shut behind him – Roy smiled.

He'd done it.

He'd get a bus into town. He'd be there at the sports centre in plenty of time. Now he had time to think about what the passport officer had said. *We don't believe a word of it.* A word of what? What did she mean by that?

Roy passed through one more door, and saw that he had got to Arrivals. The first thing he saw was dozens of people waiting for passengers to arrive, some of them holding signs with names on. Senor Bielsa. Mr Radebe. Others were holding a banner about the university.

Then he saw her.

She was staring right at him. Her face immobile. Not smiling. Not frowning.

Rocky.

Roy's first thought was that she looked like Dad.

His second thought was a question. Why is *she* here?

His third thought was back to Dad again. Something was wrong. With Dad. Why else would Rocky be meeting him at the airport when she was supposed to be playing in the game of her life in less than two hours' time?

17

'WHAT'S UP?'

'Dad's ill,' Rocky replied. 'Iller, I mean. He's okay, but in hospital again.'

Roy paused. In hospital? That didn't sound *okay*. It sounded catastrophic. Roy felt sick and dizzy, his whole body shaking.

'Why didn't you tell me? Text me?'

'Mum told me I shouldn't. I wanted to.'

Roy heard his sister's voice break. She was upset. He changed tack.

'Are we going there now?' he asked. 'To the hospital, I mean. Is that why you're here?'

Rocky shook her head. 'Visiting time's

over. Mum wanted me to tell you face-to-face. Some other people know about it and she thought you might hear it from someone else on your way home. And that they might get it wrong. Then you'd hear something that you didn't know what to...'

Rocky ran out of words. She looked at her feet.

Roy breathed in. He might as well ask the question that he wanted the answer to and that he knew quite well Rocky was expecting him to ask.

'Will he die?' His voice broke as he said it. Hot tears filled his eyes, surprising him.

His sister stared hard at him. 'No. No.' She shook her head vigorously. 'He's just had a setback. He'll recover. He's better already. A bit.'

Roy breathed in again. But shallow breaths. He hated this. His dad being ill.

Hated that everything wasn't normal and happy. Why couldn't everything just be happy?

'Look,' Rocky checked her watch. 'I need to get to the game. Mum gave me some money for a taxi so we don't have to worry about time. Let's go. We can talk in the taxi.'

'Taxi from the airport?' Roy asked. 'Can we afford it?'

'No,' Rocky laughed. 'But Mum made me...'

IT WAS ONE of those big black taxis where the driver is up front on his own and speaks to you through a microphone. Roy sat with his back to the driver, facing his sister.

'So what happened?' he asked.

'They'd come to watch me training. Mum and Dad. He was okay. In the front seat, watching through the windscreen. Then he sort of slumped in his seat and he wouldn't move, so Mum rushed him to hospital.'

'What did they say at hospital?'

'Tests. To see what it was. But he's come round a bit now. He's just really tired.'

Roy nodded. He noticed his sister was looking agitated. Like she had too much going on in her head.

'But did they say what caused it?'

'They're not sure.'

'But?'

'But nothing.' Rocky sounded cross. 'I don't know.'

'Shall I stop asking you about it?' Roy suggested.

'Yes. Just until after…'

'The game?'

'Yeah.'

Roy looked outside the taxi. They were

on the motorway now. Lorries passing them on either side. He could see planes coming into the airport, hanging in the air as if they were barely moving.

He glanced back at her sister. She didn't look like someone who was about to play in the most important game of her life.

'Want to talk about the game, then?' he asked.

Rocky shook her head.

Roy understood. Sometimes you had to find that thing inside. Not be coached or motivated. Sometimes you had to dig down deep inside and drag yourself out without anybody else's help. She knew that. He knew she knew that, too. And that he had to leave her to it, even though he was desperate to help her. She was being so nice and straight with him: not the real Rocky, the Rocky who revelled in winding him up, squirting water at him and laughing at him. He wanted that Rocky back as much as he wanted his talking walking dad back.

'One thing,' Roy said.

Rocky looked him in the eye. 'Go on.'

'I believe in you,' he said. 'I believe in you one hundred per cent.'

SOWERBY VERSUS WIBSEY was being played at the sports centre on the edge of town, on the 3G pitch. Rocky asked the taxi driver to drop them off half a mile away.

'Why?' Roy asked.

'Because I want to warm up, dumbass,' his sister told him. 'I'll run slow. You don't have to worry about keeping up.'

Roy laughed. It was the first time he'd smiled since he landed back in the UK. Rocky was being Rocky. That was a good sign. For the game *and* everything else.

They jogged along the grass beside the

dual carriageway to the sports centre, Roy's rucksack on his back. When they arrived Roy immediately looked for Ffion. He'd missed her. He checked out a group of people on the far side of the pitch and quickly realised that they were fans of the opposition.

Then he saw Ffion.

She was filling bottles of water from a tap on the outside wall of the sports centre, helped by two of her teammates.

Roy waved.

Ffion waved back.

He walked closer. 'Can I do that?' he asked.

'Please,' she said, ruffling his hair as she went past.

Roy was hoping for more than a ruffle of hair from Ffion, like a hug. But he knew she'd be one hundred per cent in game mode. He had the present in his rucksack. But now was not the time. He knew that.

'Can you bring those water bottles over to me and make sure all the girls are wearing their shin pads?' she yelled back. 'Some of them pretend to forget. Fine them a pound if they aren't wearing them. Please.'

'Sure.'

'And, er… we'll talk after, yeah?' Ffion's eyes lingered on Roy for a moment.

'Yeah. After,' Roy repeated. 'I've got you a…'

But Ffion had gone.

Roy grabbed the bottles, then walked across the 3G pitch to where Rocky and her teammates were. Ffion was standing among them, having quiet words with them one after the other. She took the water carrier off him and started to hand the bottles out.

Roy kicked his sister gently on the leg.

'Ow. Idiot,' she shouted. 'Do you want another soaking?'

Laughter from her teammates.

'Just to say good luck.' Roy stared at her.

'We don't need luck, do we girls?' Ffion interrupted the sibling row. 'We're fit. We're strong. We're prepared. We're at our best. This is a game none of us will ever forget. Yes?'

Roy was now surrounded by shouting footballers. They were standing as one. Roy felt that pre-match buzz.

Competitive football. There was nothing like it.

A minute later, the referee blew her whistle to summon the teams.

Ffion handed Roy a clipboard. 'Keep this. Write down anything you see that we can work on in the second half. I'm doing the half time talk, but I need your eyes. Okay?'

'Yes, boss,' Roy said.

Ffion smiled. 'Hey,' she said in a quiet

voice. 'Is Rocky going to be okay with everything... you know... your dad? I find her hard to read.'

Roy looked at his sister, then back at Ffion.

'I think she's right where she needs to be,' he grinned. 'I think she's going to smash it, Ffion.'

As he spoke, Roy noticed his sister look away quickly. He wondered if she'd heard him. He wondered if she was happy with what he'd said.

19

THE GAME BEGAN with both teams sounding each other out, careful not to make any mistakes that could lead to a goal being given away. There was so much riding on the next ninety minutes that most of the players from Sowerby – and their opponents, Wibsey Warriors – were being cautious.

But there was lots of shouting, both teams communicating well, warning each other of incoming tackles. Roy knew Ffion insisted on this: she hated teams that played in silence.

One player, Roy noticed, was not being cautious.

Rocky.

If Sowerby didn't have the ball, Rocky was pressing her opponents, like a terrier snapping at their heels. If Sowerby had the ball, she was making short runs into space, calling for it, desperate to take the game to Wibsey. Roy couldn't help but smile as he watched his sister from the touchline. Then, he noticed a woman edging closer to him, like she wanted to ask him something.

Roy had learned to wait until someone spoke to him when this happened, and to always be friendly. Coach had impressed it on the players: you represent the club; be at your best.

'Thinking about all that money?' the woman asked during a break in play.

Roy knew this was trouble. More trouble. What had the passport officer said to him? *We don't believe a word of it.*

He decided to be careful. 'I'm not sure,' he laughed. 'What do you mean?'

'The Tynecaster millions.'

'Sorry? I don't...'

'She means you signing for that lot on the other side of town.' A man was with the woman now. Dark haired, with a dark look in his eyes.

'I'm not,' Roy said, indignant, taking his eyes off the pitch as his sister charged down a shot.

Then Roy heard shouting from the pitch.

Rocky was on the floor, two Wibsey players standing over her, as a third lay writhing in pain.

The referee was there in a second. She waited for Rocky to stand, then held up a yellow card.

Roy was annoyed he'd not seen the tackle. Ffion would want his view on it – and he'd missed it. He didn't want to let her down. Roy watched as the couple who'd been hassling him walked away. He could see them with another group of players' parents, pointing at Roy.

What *was* going on? Why would they *still* think he was leaving? And to Tynecaster? It was laughable.

The first half ended 0-0. Very tight. Very tense.

Apart from Rocky putting it about, there was nothing to speak about. Roy silently delivered water to every player as they slumped on the touchline. He watched Ffion as she gathered her thoughts for her team talk. This was her call. Although he had his own ideas about how to change it.

'So… we're holding them. We're matching them,' Ffion began. 'We're as good as them. Agreed?'

The Sowerby team nodded.

'No,' Ffion shook her head. 'We're *better* than them. But we're letting them think they're containing us, that they can just score one and win it.'

More nods. Roy watched Ffion take a deep breath.

'You know that TV advert that says that cats need to be "more dog"?' Ffion asked.

None of the girls seemed to have heard

of it.

Ffion shrugged. 'Well, there's this cat. It's a bit passive, a bit pathetic. Then it starts to act like a dog, chasing sticks, being just... more fun. Immediately it's more effective. It gets things done. It's less cat, more dog. Be more dog.'

Ffion paused.

'Not quite getting you, Coach,' Molly Power, the Sowerby fullback, called out.

Ffion looked at Rocky, then at the rest of her team. 'I need...' she said in a serious voice, 'I need you to hassle them, take risks, attack them. We lose this and we'll be feeling bad for a year, until we get another chance. I want you all to *be more Rocky*. Okay?'

The energy among the players had changed now. They were staring into each others' eyes. Tight-jawed. Some of them standing. Others grinning.

'You remember when Rovers won that play-off two months ago?'

More nods. Several of the players looking at Roy.

'This is our play-off. This is our chance. Now go and win it.'

Roy gathered the team's water bottles as the players took their positions on the pitch. Ffion came to stand with him and gazed over at the group that had been hassling Roy.

'That lot. They think you're leaving,' she told him. 'There've been rumours. While you were away. Cleaver didn't deny it. You and Paco, the word is.'

Roy frowned. 'I see.'

'Well?' Ffion asked. 'Is it true?'

'No,' Roy snapped. It was the first time he'd ever said anything tense to Ffion.

'Promise?'

'What is this?' Roy asked. He was still

angry. But he knew now it wasn't about him. It was about Sowerby and Ffion and Rocky.

'Forget me,' he said. 'I'm not leaving. I promise. You need to keep your mind on this game. You need,' Roy smirked, 'to be more Rocky.'

20

THE SECOND HALF was different, the calm caution of the first half gone. Now that Sowerby were going hard up against Wibsey, Wibsey were doing the same back. Everything had changed.

Tackles flying in.

Fouls.

Yellow cards.

In-your-face arguments.

And – because of the new intensity – there were goal chances. Both teams hit the post in the first fifteen of the second half. Both teams had penalty claims waved away.

It was face to face, end to end, box to box.

Roy stood on the touchline, watching intently, trying to analyse the game to see if he could work out the puzzle that it had become. He could hear Ffion calling out orders, tweaking her formation, switching players' positions. Ffion was so on top of the game. Tactically. Technically. Motivationally. And all that while she was playing too.

Roy had no idea how she did it. She really was something else.

But, with twenty minutes to go, players on both sides tiring, Ffion ran over to him, taking the chance to speak.

'I need you to get my inhaler from the car. It's open. Okay?'

Roy nodded, and jogged over to Ffion's car. As he passed the group of Wibsey fans, he heard more boos, some of them pointing at him.

So annoying.

So irritating.

What with this game and not really knowing what was going on with Dad, he felt himself being overcome with anger. That rage from deep down that he sometimes felt. But now was not the time to challenge them. He knew that. In fact, he could hear Johnny Dexter's advice.

Leave it. Don't engage. Think about what you need to think about here and now.

So, Roy put his darker thoughts aside. He grabbed the inhaler from Ffion's car and jogged back towards to his place on the touchline.

It happened when he was halfway between the car and the pitch side.

Ffion glanced up, then fired a long diagonal ball out to the wing and Molly

Power. Power was running through the tired Wibsey midfield, level with their defence, who were still playing a high offside to catch Sowerby out.

Roy knew she'd spotted something. A weakness.

Molly took the ball down with one touch, waited for Ffion to time her run, then poked

a slide rule ball into the box. Ffion broke free of the defence.

On side.

In on goal.

One touch to put the keeper on the floor.

A second touch to roll the ball into the net.

GOAL!

The shout from players around the pitch was so loud, a car alarm went off behind Roy.

But, as the players came to congratulate Ffion, he saw her calming them down, looking them in the eye. Talking. She was thinking ahead. And he could read her mind. They could celebrate later. First they needed to make sure they had something *to* celebrate.

Following the restart, Wibsey were giving it everything. They could see clearly what they had to lose now. They immediately looked stronger. Dangerous.

As the clock clicked down, Sowerby were defending deeper and deeper.

The pressure was intense.

Ffion was booked for shouldering a Wibsey player off the ball as she broke down the wing. Then another Sowerby player was yellow-carded for a push.

And then, to Roy's relief, a Sowerby attack, the Wibsey team back-peddling to keep up, but Roy could see they didn't have the legs. They were shattered.

Then, dramatically, the attack fizzled out and Wibsey won the ball back, their central midfielder hammering a hopeful pass forward. The rest, to Roy, seemed to play out in slow motion. The Sowerby defence was caught flat-footed. The Wibsey substitute broke through, her fresh legs taking her clear. Only Rocky had a chance of catching her before she reached the penalty area.

But Rocky was behind the sub, not alongside her. There was no way she could clean-tackle. With only the keeper to beat, the Wibsey sub prepared to strike the ball, just as Rocky lunged in, taking her legs.

A howl of outrage from the side-line. From the Wibsey families.

'REFEREEEEEEEE!!!!!'

And there she was. The referee. Standing over Rocky, a red card in the air.

Roy watched his sister climb up off the floor, ignore a push from one of the Wibsey players, and walk towards him. And, as she came closer, Roy could see that she was grinning.

Roy handed his sister a bottle of water.

Rocky's eyes sparkled as she took a deep breath and said: 'And that – dear brother – is called taking one for the team.'

FIVE MINUTES LATER – to the boos of the Wibsey fans, and more pushing from their players – the Sowerby squad were jumping up and down in the centre circle. Rocky raced off the touchline to join her teammates the moment she saw the referee put her whistle

to her lips. They'd done it. They were in the pyramid. At the foot of the pyramid, but it meant, if they could keep winning, slowly, but surely, Sowerby could work their way up – maybe one day – to the top.

Later, when her players were in the dressing rooms and they were alone, Roy gave Ffion a hug. Then he put his hand into his rucksack.

'I got you something,' he said, pulling out a small box.

Ffion stepped back, shaking her head, her eyes wild with panic.

'What?' Roy said.

Then he felt himself flush deep red. No. She'd misunderstood.

Stuttering, he said. 'It's a stone. Just a stone. From the top of the Arctic mountains. I found it and bought this box for it. Look.'

Ffion opened the small box and grinned.

She took the stone out, admiring how the floodlights made the seams of gold sparkle. 'I love it,' she said, kissing him.

21

BACK HOME, AFTER giving Roy a silent hug, Mum made a fuss of Rocky, fed her and ran her a bubble bath. While they were upstairs Roy sat in the front room, his eyes wide open staring at the dark skies outside the window, then the pile of bills and bank statements on the table.

He felt weird.

The room was empty. Just Roy. No Dad.

Dad's wheelchair was there. Empty. Roy stared at it and felt a deep longing to see his father. And he would. At the hospital, at exactly 10 a.m. tomorrow morning. Then he'd feel a lot better. Just to see he was okay. Just to see him, be with him, be normal again.

But sitting here, now, next to the space where his dad usually was when they watched the football or played FIFA together, did not feel good.

After a few minutes Mum came in.

'So how was the tour?' she smiled. She was tired.

'Fine,' Roy said. 'Tell me about Dad.'

Mum let out a long and deep sigh. 'He's quite a bit better, really. But it was scary when he had his turn. They said something changed in his brain. It's made him less mobile for a while, but he seems more with it. I don't know, Roy. I won't lie. For a while I thought it was very serious.'

'And how about you?' Roy wanted to know.

'Me?'

'Yes, how are you?'

'I'm fine, Roy. Physically.' Mum hesitated for a few seconds, casting her eyes around the room. The table. The wheelchair. The family photos on the fireplace. 'Just... well... there's some things we need to talk about. But it can wait until tomorrow. You must be shattered. Tell me about the Arctic.'

Roy shook his head. 'That can wait,

Mum. Let's talk about the things we need to talk about now.'

Mum smiled and studied Roy for a few seconds. Roy kept quiet. This felt serious. He really had no idea what she was going to say.

'I am going to have to give up my jobs,' Mum started.

'All of them?'

'Yes.'

'Right.'

'We'll get some help from the government,' Mum explained. 'But it's not as much as I was earning. And nowhere near enough to...'

'It's fine, Mum,' Roy interrupted: he didn't want her to have to ask him for money.

'And we'll need some specialist equipment. Like a winch and some other things, so I can move your dad when you're away.'

'You can have everything I earn,' Roy said. 'Every penny.'

'That's not fair, Roy. But we will need…
well… most of… some of it. I'm sorry, Roy.
You're a young man…'

'And you're my mum,' Roy said, feeling a
burst of emotion. 'And he's my dad.'

Mum nodded. 'You're a good boy.'

Roy scratched his head. 'But it'll still be
tight,' he said. He glanced at the pile of bills
and bank statements on the table next to the
window. 'I earn £800 a week. How long will
it take us to save up for the extra equipment
we need?'

'I don't know. It'll be tight for a while,'
Mum said. 'But, once Dad gets a bit better, I
can go back to work. And Rocky's growing
up. She's been a good girl. We could send her
out to work, too.'

Roy laughed.

But only because he didn't really know
what to say. There were too many questions

running through his mind. What if Dad didn't get better? What if Mum couldn't go back to work? What if he was side-lined at Melchester Rovers? Where would the money come from then?

22

Just before he arrived at the hospital, the next morning, Roy's phone vibrated.

It was a text from Johnny Dexter.

Roy. Please come in ASAP.

Roy texted back.

Just going in to see Dad. Hospital. Give me an hour.

Roy turned his phone off, pocketed it and walked along a windowless corridor, the smell of disinfectant sharp in his nostrils, the lights bright, hurting his tired eyes.

Roy didn't wait for a reply from Coach. He didn't need permission to see his dad on his day off. Why did Coach want to see him on a day off, anyway? Things were weird with Johnny Dexter now. But worrying about all that was for later.

Dad was in a small ward with three other men. One of them was coughing so much his family pulled a curtain round the bed for privacy. Two children waiting outside the next ward pointed at Roy and stared. Roy smiled at them. Then he went in to see his dad.

Dad raised his right hand when he saw Roy.

'How are you feeling?' Roy sat down.

Dad's bed was made of white metal tubes, with a winch above it, so that the doctors and nurses could move him.

Danny Race put a thumb up. Roy studied his face. His eyes. He could tell a lot from his dad's eyes. Now his dad had hardly any words it was the best way of reading him. They were still red; but maybe less than they had been.

Roy decided to talk about what needed talking about first. His dad had always been honest and direct; he hated leaving things unsaid. Roy would do the same for him now.

'Mum says you've lost some mobility?' Roy said.

Dad nodded.

'Me and Mum talked last night. It's going to be okay. Mum's going to give up her jobs for a bit. Until you recover. I'm getting paid more now we got promoted to League One. It'll be tight, but we can manage.'

Dad half-smiled.

'Norway?' he said.

Roy beamed. A word. A fantastic word.

'You want to know how it was?'

'Yes.'

Roy began to tell his dad about the tour. The good stuff. The goals. The mountains. The Scandinavian fans. As he spoke he couldn't help but feel excited. Two words from his dad in the space of a few seconds. That was amazing. He wondered whether Mum had noticed Dad was talking more since he'd had to go to hospital. Or was this just a one-off? He told his dad about the football, then the Arctic hare and the 24/7 daylight. He did his best to make it sound interesting and fun.

'But?' Dad said when he finished.

Roy was stunned. Three words? What was happening? He decided not to go on about it. He'd answer Dad's questions. Dad had sensed something wasn't quite right amid all the excitement.

'There was some weirdness,' he said. 'Coach had me on the bench, then left me out on the wing. It was like he didn't want me involved.'

Dad rubbed his chin slowly, his hand lingering there as if he'd forgotten what he was doing.

'But then he went off,' Roy lowered his voice, so that no-one else on the ward could hear. 'With Cleaver. And that agent.'

Roy watched Dad's face cloud over. Dad hated Cleaver as much as Roy did.

'And now he wants me at Mel Park. After I've seen you. But we're meant to be having three days off. It's all kind of weird.'

Dad tried to speak, leaning forward, but the words he was looking for didn't come. He fell back onto his pillows, frustrated.

A nurse arrived at the end of the bed.

'Some tests,' he said, checking a clipboard. 'I'm sorry, Roy. I'm going to have to ask you to go.'

Roy stood up. It was bizarre how everyone seemed to know his name. Something else he had to get used to.

But Dad beckoned him over. Roy hoped for more words as he leant down to his dad and gave him a kiss on his head. Dad took the opportunity to grab Roy's arm and squeeze it hard. So hard it hurt. But it was pain Roy welcomed. He loved it that his dad was strong enough to do that.

He was pretty sure the vice-like grip meant look after yourself, don't let yourself be treated badly.

Roy looked deep into his dad's eyes. 'I'll be careful,' he said. 'I've signed a contract for next season already. It's all going to be okay.'

But – as he walked out of the hospital doors – deep down Roy felt worried that all the weirdness of the last few days with Johnny Dexter was about to come to a head.

23

ROY JOGGED ALONG the canal from the hospital to Mel Park. He put up his hood to maintain a bit of anonymity so that he could have some time to think about his dad.

Dad was weaker, less mobile. That was true.

But he seemed to have more words.

Things were always changing. Roy was coming to understand that. When he was a kid – before Dad was ill, before Melchester Rovers – things were the same, normal, predictable. Now Roy couldn't say what was going to happen from one day to the next.

Off the pitch and on it.

The canal was a little low after the hot summer, but there were still boats cruising up and down, two of them queuing at the locks. The canal headed straight into the city centre, to its industrial heartland, but there was a shortcut into the stadium car park if you scrambled up a bank and worked your

way through a few yards of brambles and round a clump of trees.

Which is exactly what Roy did.

Once he was in the car park he brushed himself down to see a cluster of people standing by a familiar, flash Aston Martin.

Instinctively Roy recoiled, took a step backwards and moved behind a tree. The car belonged to Alan Talbot. Roy didn't like Talbot. The times he had met him before, Talbot had called him Rod all the time, then tried to make out he knew all about his career. And Roy still had no idea why he'd been in Norway.

Talbot was a phoney. Roy knew that.

Roy scanned the group of people again.

Yes, he knew them all.

Alan Talbot, football agent.

Barry Cleaver, owner of Melchester Rovers.

Johnny Dexter, Coach.

And, Roy's teammate, Paco Diaz.

Roy had no choice but to walk across the car park and find out what this was all about.

Johnny Dexter spotted Roy first and walked towards him. Coach spoke quietly so that none of the others hear.

'Roy. Thanks for coming. How's your dad?'

'Mixed,' Roy said. 'What's this?'

'This,' Coach sighed, a shadow passing over his face as he looked down at his feet, 'is what I was telling you about in Tromsø, Roy.'

'What you *weren't* telling me about, you mean?'

'Yes,' Coach frowned. 'That.'

'You still can't tell me?'

'I can't, Roy. I have just realised I have absolutely no idea what is going on.'

Roy glanced over Johnny Dexter's shoulder and saw Barry Cleaver, eyes sparkling, and a sharkish grin on his face.

'YOU'RE NOT SERIOUS!' Johnny Dexter boomed.

They were in Cleaver's office now. The door was closed, and Roy felt trapped. He watched as Barry Cleaver smiled, stared back at Coach, and lit a huge cigar.

Alan Talbot remained outside, speaking into his phone.

Roy felt desperate to tell the chairman that you weren't allowed to smoke indoors. He decided against it. For now. But there was something more serious than smoke in the air: there was what Cleaver had just told them.

177

'I own Melchester Rovers, Johnny Dexter. I am Barry – The Meat – Cleaver. Meat products impresario extraordinaire! I was BORN serious. Very tidy offer I have received from Tynecaster for these two lads here: Paco Diaz and Roy Race. And who am I to stand in the way of talented youngsters having the chance to play in the Champions League? Would be selfish of me to say no...'

Roy just couldn't take it in. What was happening to him?

Johnny moved closer to Cleaver and glared at him.

'These lads have just done a miracle and helped Melchester Rovers get promoted,' Dexter raged. 'They've given hope to our fans for the first time in years! They're our future! And you're going to sell them?'

'*Have* sold them,' another voice added. Alan Talbot was in the room now. 'Just off the phone with Tynecaster's Director of Football, Bazza. All sorted. A cool mill for the Spanish winger, £500,000 for Rod Race. And they'll be on five times what they're on now.'

'Roy,' Johnny snapped.

'What?' Alan Talbot stepped backwards, his shoulder hitting the door. The agent winced in pain.

'ROY Race. Not Rod. And that Spanish winger is a decent kid called Paco Diaz. Not a cut of beef.'

'Okay,' Talbot whimpered.

Roy sat and watched the conversation play out in silence. He didn't even look at Paco. It was like he was watching his life change on a film and there was nothing he could do about it.

'Didn't you hear what Alan said, Dexter?' Cleaver cackled. 'The deal is done. COMPRONDE!'

Roy stood up, stepped forward. 'No,' he said. 'It's not.'

'Eh?'

Roy's heart was hammering so much he felt sick. He was thinking about the girl he'd met with her dad on the first day of pre-season training, the woman at airport passport control, the nurse in the hospital. Ffion. His dad. All those people he'd made a promise to. He had to speak out.

'We have to sign a contract,' Roy said. 'Or no deal. We're not slaves.'

Paco stepped forward to be shoulder to shoulder with Roy.

'Absolutely, my friend,' Paco said, but his wavering voice betrayed his nervousness. 'Mr Cleaver, thank you for this kind offer. We will discuss with our families and...'

'YOU ARE SOLD! UNDERSTAND ME? GOT IT!' Cleaver raged. 'YOU'RE

NOTHING! A BUNCH OF NOTHING KIDS! KIDS THAT I OWN! SO IF I SAY YOU'RE GONE, YOU ARE GONE!'

Roy watched in horror as Johnny grabbed at Cleaver.

'Talk to them like that again, Barry...' he ranted. 'And I'll remember why I used to get all them red cards. Why they called me "the Hard Man".'

This was too much for Roy. He knew that – whatever someone has done to you – violence was wrong. Cleaver could get hurt. Johnny could end up in prison. He had to stop it.

But how?

ROY PUT HIS hand on Johnny's arm. His muscles felt like rock. Like the cold hard impenetrable rock of the Arctic mountains.

'Coach, don't,' he said quietly. 'You'll get in trouble. It's not right.'

Roy felt Johnny's arm relax.

'You're ALREADY in trouble,' Cleaver laughed. 'You're fired, Johnny Dexter.'

Coach fell away from Roy now, back into his seat. His face ashen.

'You hear me?' Cleaver gloated, leaning forward, as Alan Talbot also sat forward in his seat like a ringside fan at a boxing bout.

'You're finished at Melchester Rovers,' Cleaver went on. 'Done.'

Johnny Dexter spoke calmly, quietly. His eyes were more thoughtful than enraged now. Roy could see the bigger man emerging.

'First, you almost killed Mighty Mouse and now this with the kids?' Coach began. 'I love this club but... I can't work for you no more. Fire me if you want but, regardless... I quit.'

The room was silent. Johnny Dexter took the opportunity to move next to Roy and speak to him and Paco.

'I feared this was coming,' he said quietly. 'But, I'm sorry, so sorry... I was under contract not to tell you anything,' he muttered. 'I tried to stop it. I tried... but if I'd have told you I might have been sacked and gone to jail and the club would have been left without me or Mouse. I had no choice. But now...'

Johnny Dexter's voice faded to nothing.

But now? Roy thought.

Now?

What?

25

ROY RAN HOME via the Terrible Two Hundred, a set of steps from the bus station on the edge of town up to the Moor, where he used to play pretty much all his football. For Grimroyd.

It would be the Moor Cup in a few days, Roy remembered. Simpler times, he thought. Maybe it had been better then?

There was a storm brewing, a strong warm wind whipping in from the west. More and more intense as he ran up the steps without stopping, pushing himself so hard his lungs and legs and head hurt. Roy liked it. He remembered at school when it was windy: everyone went a little crazy.

When Roy got to the top he jogged over to the cluster of trees that hung over the edge of the moortop down to the town.

He sat and gazed out across Melchester. This was the spot he'd sat with that evening with Lofty Peak, when Lofty had said he'd given up football for good.

But Lofty had left Tynecaster to end up at Melchester. And he was happy now.

Roy knew very well what he wanted to do about Barry Cleaver's offer. But he had promised himself he would go to the Moor alone and weigh it up, before he went home.

His choice was a simple one. Or had been.

Stay at Melchester Rovers, the club he and his family had loved for generations with a coach he trusted. Help it become the force it used to be in English game by playing every week. Make Melchester great again. Remain Roy of the Rovers.

Or.

Leave.

Join the team he hated. Tynecaster; Melchester's greatest rivals. Break all those promises he'd made to people who had been badgering him all week.

I'm not leaving: I promise.

I'm one hundred per cent Melchester Rovers, me.

Why would he leave? Seriously, why?

There was one reason.

Money.

Roy had not forgotten what Barry Cleaver had said about money. That he would earn five times as much at Tynecaster.

Money was nothing to Roy. Not really.

But money would help make his mum's life a thousand times easier. And his dad's.

Then there was Coach. Johnny Dexter. He'd gone, anyway. The man Roy looked up to nearly as much as he looked up to his own dad.

Roy put his head in his hands, then stared hard into the wind.

'I'm Melchester Rovers,' Roy yelled.

Then he stood up, facing into the storm

that was coming hard across the tops now. Heavy raindrops hitting him in the face. He relished it.

Because he'd made his mind up.

He knew what he was going to do.

ROY OF THE ROVERS.

THE FIRST SEASON

Keep track of every new *Roy of the Rovers* book here!
Don't forget to tick the boxes as you read each one.

FICTION

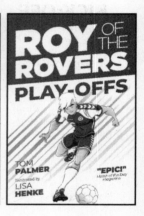

BOOK 1
SCOUTED

Author: Tom Palmer
Out: October 2018
ISBN: 978-1-78108-698-8

Roy Race is the most talented striker in Melchester – but is he good enough to catch the eye of the Melchester Rovers scouts?

READ? ☐

BOOK 2
TEAMWORK

Author: Tom Palmer
Out: February 2019
ISBN: 978-1-78108-707-7

Life gets tricky for Roy as he adjusts to life in the spotlight. Fortune and glory await, but can Roy juggle football, fame and family?

READ? ☐

BOOK 3
PLAY-OFFS

Author: Tom Palmer
Out: May 2019
ISBN: 978-1-78108-722-0

Crunch time for Rovers: the end of the season is here, the club is in deep trouble, and it's down to Roy to bring a bit of hope back to the Melchester faithful.

READ? ☐

COMICS

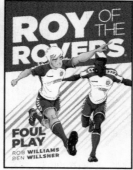

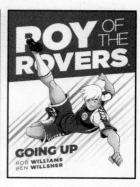

BOOK 1
KICK-OFF

Writer: Rob Williams
Artist: Ben Willsher
Out: November 2018
ISBN: 978-1-78108-652-0

Roy Race is 16, talented,
and desperate to make
it as a footballer. But
is he good enough for
Melchester Rovers?
Now's the time to prove
if he's got what it takes to
become Roy of the Rovers.

READ? ☐

BOOK 2
FOUL PLAY

Writer: Rob Williams
Artist: Ben Willsher
Out: March 2019
ISBN: 978-1-78108-669-8

Roy picks up an injury
that puts him on the
sidelines, and suddenly
there's competition for
his place as a brand new
- and brilliant - striker
is brought in by the
management...

READ? ☐

BOOK 3
GOING UP

Writer: Rob Williams
Artist: Ben Willsher
Out: June 2019
ISBN: 978-1-78108-673-5

Roy and the team have
battled through a tough
season, but have they
got enough left to get
promoted? Or will they fall
at the final hurdle and see
the club sold by its greedy
owner?

READ? ☐

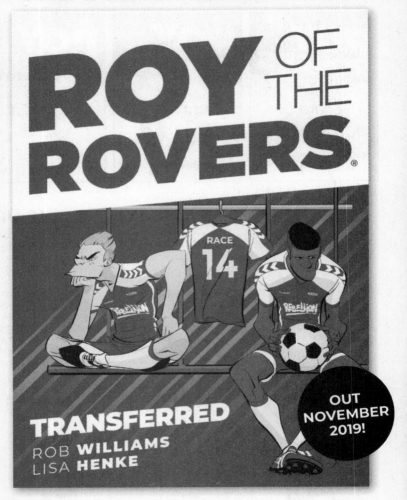